Clint Faraday Mysteries
#16
*The Time Factor*

A call about trouble between neighbors – but the caller was dead at the time the call was received. Blah people in town. Too blah to believe.

Clint Faraday Mysteries
#16
***The Time Factor***

## Contents

# About the author

CD was born in Lakeland, Florida. His education is in genetics and botany. He has traveled over much of the world, particularly when he was in music as a rock rhythm guitarist with some well-known bands in the late sixties and early seventies. He has worked as a high steel worker and as a longshoreman, clerk, orchidist, bar owner, salvage yard manager and landscaper – among other things.

CD began writing fiction in 1984 and has more than 115 books published as of this time in SciFi, murder, orchid culture and various other fields.

He now resides in Bocas del Toro and David, Panamá, where he continues research into epiphytic plants. He loves the culture of the indigenous people and counts a majority of his closer friends among that group. Several have "adopted" him as their father. He funds those he can afford through the universities where they have all excelled. "The Indios are very intelligent people, they are simply too poor (in material things and money. Culturally, they are very wealthy) to pursue higher education."

CD loves Panamá and the people. He plans to spend the rest of his life in the paradise that is Panamá
- Estrelita Suarez V.


CD is involved in research of natural cancer cure at this time. It has proven effective in all cases, so far. It is based on a plant that has been in use for thousands of years, is safe, available, and cheap. He has studied botany, and was cured of a serious lymphoma with use of the plant, *Ambrosia peruviana.*

Information about this cure is free on the FaceBook page, Ambrosia peruviana for cancer. CD asks only that all who try it please report on its effectiveness on that group.

Clint Faraday #16
*** The Time Factor ***

<u>*Prologue*</u>

Clint Faraday, retired PI from Florida, USA, now living in Bocas del Toro, Panamá, brought in the corvina, a nice one, and put it in the bait well with the other he caught only a few minutes earlier. That would be enough fish for now. He decided to see if there were any langosta of a decent size at the mouth of the pass between the Zapatillas, then he'd laze around a bit, then maybe go home.

He started the engine and headed out toward the pass when his cellular buzzed, so he answered. It was Sergio Sanchez, captain of the police in Bocas Town, who Clint often worked with. Clint was retired (Hah!), but was back in the detective business only a couple of weeks after moving to Panamá, six years ago. The cases here were different, and looked at from a somewhat different perspective than in the states.

"Buenos!" Clint greeted. "Que pasa?"

"Hi, Clint. We seem to be having quite a bit of trouble from that John Benton character and the Sanders. Sandy and Herb. Benton called to say they were threatening him because his horse got into their garden and ruined something or other. He says they opened the gate themselves. He's not responsible for anything if they left the gate from his property open – with which I agree.

"He said to tell you they were sneaking around your house and Judi's (Clint's attractive nextdoor neighbor, who helped him in a lot of his cases). He doesn't trust them since that incident with the missing TV."

"When was this?" Clint asked. "The call from him?"

"About five minutes ago. Four thirty three on the book."

"I don't picture him ever calling you. Not John. He might smack Herb in the puss, which he needs, at times. He wouldn't call you."

"His voice? It was him, I'm sure. No one else has that raspy a voice around here. You can listen to the recording. I already sent Jorge and Gino over to see what's happening. I just wanted to tell you about the sneaking around your place."

"I don't see Herb or Sandy sneaking around my place or anyone else's. Something big must have happened to make him call you that he isn't talking about."

"I agree there! I was ... wait a moment. Jorge is calling on the radio ... great lord! Benton is dead! His head's nearly cut off his body!"

"I'll be there as fast as this rig will make it!"

Chapter one

He made it to Bocas in sixteen minutes, which was good for his rig. He tied to the police dock and went into the office to find that Sergio had gone to Benton's place. It was close to Clint's, so he got in his boat and went around to tie to his own deck. He could walk the six or seven blocks to Benton's house (if they had blocks on that road).

Judi (Judi Lum), his attractive neighbor who helped him with a lot of his cases, was waiting for him, and said Sergio had called her to tell him Doc had come up with something strange.

"Strange?"

"Yes. Something about him being dead for more than an hour. Probably more like an hour and a half. Maybe that means something to you?"

"Yeah! He called Sergio less than half an hour ago!"

"I see." Nobody ever said Judi was slow. She walked along with him to Benton's place. Half the police department was there, it seemed. It was a rather strange conglomeration of police and Doc's crew. Doc was the ME for Isla Colón. Sergio met Clint, and said it was the kind of thing that he seemed interested in. He had always helped the police when asked, and they might need his experience with this kind of thing. It was rare in Bocas to have murders. This one was more than a bit puzzling.

Oh. There were two reporters who liked to hammer at the police there. If Clint just showed up and started doing anything or asking questions they would print that he was intruding into the legal investigation, and the police had enough of a problem when they had to actually solve a case – or something worse. This made it plain that his help as an expert was requested.

"What's this crap about him being dead awhile before he called your office about it?" Clint asked when the reporters were enough of a distance away that they couldn't hear.

"I can let you hear the recording. I could have sworn that it was Benton's voice, and even his phrasing. I talked to Sandy and Herb, and they said there wasn't any problem with him about his horse, or anything else. They'd gotten along well enough since they made it plain to him they weren't backing down and letting him intimidate them like some of these spineless gringo wimps do, or something. You can talk to them. if you like. They're out back, and Jorge is questioning them about people being seen looking into the houses in the area. So far, they haven't known anything at all about any of the things Benton was supposedly complaining about.

"You know how I can tell a disguised voice, Clint. This one fooled me."

"It does tell us one very important thing," Clint said. "Whoever it was is someone who knew him and the people around here pretty damned well!"

"Yes. They would have to be around him to know the phrasing he would use."

"But there's another little detail we probably should consider. They haven't been around him for the past month or so."

Sergio thought for a minute, started a shrug, then brightened. "Ah! They didn't know that the trouble with Sandy and Herb was resolved!"

Clint nodded, then said he was going to nose around a

bit. He'd go to the station later to listen to the recording of the phony complaint. He might be able to catch something.

He looked over the outside, found nothing out of place, then went inside. Doc had the body on the Gurney for transport. Clint opened the bag and took a quick look-see, then said it was someone pretty powerful to cut that much with one swing, with which Doc agreed. "Also tall. The cut was slightly downward from the side. Benton was only five eight or nine, but this one will be over six feet."

"That reduces the suspect list to only five thousand people here on the isla," Clint replied – which got him the finger. He said he would look over the place as soon as the CSI team left. They'd be there for another three or four hours. Clint knew forensic science procedures as well or better than the team. He'd be damned careful not to damage anything that could be called evidence. Clint pointed to the two reporters. Doc grinned, and called, "Okay boys! Transport! I'll want to know a few answers about this one, so be careful. I have the equipment at the morgue to find what I don't understand about this pretty fast. Go, people! The trail grows stale!"

He grinned and winked to Clint, and headed outside. The reporters were crowding around him (as much as three people can crowd anyone). He was telling them he had to have some equipment to answer a question or two, and he wasn't about to stick his neck out through stupid speculation. He'd leave that kind of thing to them. He said it in a good-natured way, but many a truth is spoken in jest. They'd follow him back to the morgue and hang around as long as he wanted. He'd call for some odd piece of equipment, swear, and go back into the lab. The reporters would wait. He'd drop a few tidbits about "... the time factor, it has to be about the time factor!" or something, and they'd die of curiosity. Clint already knew what that would be about.

Clint waited until the van and the reporters had left, then went over the house and murder room carefully. The forensics team was good. They hadn't missed anything he could find.

He soon went out and to the police station. Judi had been talking with the neighbors the whole time. She was a genius about getting information people didn't know they'd given. She walked back to his place with him. All she'd learned was that there were three or four men and a woman who had been hanging around the past two days. One of the men had been here before, maybe six or eight months ago, and had been on what seemed to be friendly terms with Benton. They were just normal people.

"They big?" Clint asked.

"Well, two are tall. They played soccer and basketball when they were here before. They may have been Panamanian. They seemed Latino, at least. At least a couple of them spoke English, and all of them spoke decent Spanish. Not exactly Panamanian Spanish, but very good. They would sometimes speak in English when they weren't including a native.

"Some people say they were all here, some say only the one. I think they stayed in town, and the one came here with Benton before. This time, they all came a couple of times, and the one by himself, once, that they knew about. They didn't see any of them today."

"I imagine they were careful *not* to be seen," Clint said. "I'll have to find them. Quietly. We don't want anyone to know I'm even looking for them."

"I figured. I let them tell me all kinds of things without asking anything."

"I know your method. It works once in five times with me. It always works with you."

"Not always! I've told you fifty billion times not to exaggerate!"

They laughed and chatted, Clint got his moto out and headed for town. He wanted to know which one of them was a good mimic, too.


Sergio set the recording to the time received. Benton's voice came on asking for him. "Yes. Go ahead."

"This is John Benton, on the Saigon road."

"Yes?"

"I gotta ask you to get those lousy damned jaw-flapper Sanders slugs off my back! They even had the damned balls to threaten me because my horse got in their flower garden! Hell, they left the gate open themselves! It ain't no fault'a mine if they leave the damned gate open themselves! Back to home the heat would arrest *them*!

"They was sneakin' around my place and that Clint guy's place at night, his and that Chink woman right next door to his place. They done threatened to slice me up if I don't pay for their dam flowers or somethin' like. You gotta *do* somethin' about those shits!"

It went on like that for about a minute. Sergio said he'd send a man over to warn them to stay off his property. Clint had smirked at two spots, making Sergio deeply thoughtful. He suddenly brightened.

"Themselves?"

"Uh-huh. He would always say 'hisself' and 'theirselfs'

when he was ranting about someone.”

“I should have caught that. I’ll have to give myself a severe reprimand for shirking my duty!”

They talked a bit about the case. Clint said he had a little information to check out. He’d be in touch as soon as he learned anything. It was hard to picture someone like Benton being involved in anything that would get him killed.

Chapter two

Clint would have to start from nothing here, really. What he knew about Benton was next to nothing. He hadn't cared for the ass from the first time they met at El Toro Loco, when he had just moved down there from the states. Benton had inherited the place when his spinster aunt died, being her only living relative. From the things he knew about her, he could deduce she had moved to Bocas Town mainly to get away from him and his friends in Mississippi or Missouri or somewhere in that area. He was a typical redneck – which Clint had enough of to last a lifetime from a few recent cases. Of all the places a redneck shouldn't come, Panamá was near the top of the list, and Bocas del Toro, Panamá, was on top, or as close to the top as could be imagined.

That could be behind this. It looked, from the way he was sliced, that there was a lot of emotion behind the swing. Clint wanted to know about the three or four men and a woman.

Bob, at the Golden Grill, knew the woman's name was Lucia Aumond. She was recently from Louisiana, but was born in Panamá, in the canal zone. Her father was a gringo from the states. One of the men she had called Lyle. He was the closest to a gringo in looks. Lucia had a good figure, but a more-or-less plain face. Lyle was about six two, 250, or a few more pounds. They were all staying at the Olas. They weren't popular with the gringos or the natives, though they weren't necessarily unpopular. Sort of neutral. People didn't seek them out, but they didn't avoid them, either.

"They're just sorta ... there, if you know what I mean," Billy explained. "You know the type. Sort of background figures. Like, 'We were sitting on the deck and he came out and nodded. I don't remember when he left' sort of thing. The kind of people you don't really notice. I doubt I could describe any of them very much. Two men who were sort of mousy and two who were fairly tall – I think. Even that's like trying to bring it up from the haze.

"You think they were mixed up in the Benton thing?

"I don't suppose he'll be greatly missed. He could be an ass, but that was the way he was raised. It's not entirely his fault. He's just being his Poppa. Lots like that in the states, particularly the Ozarks and surroundings and down through central Florida. Very cliquish. Ten friends and fifty enemies. That's why I can't believe any of those five did it. They're the type who don't have real friends or real enemies. That's *all* he had, so they just wouldn't fit."

The others nodded agreement. Clint said that was sort of his impression. There just wasn't anyone else around who fit the picture of his killer, either. He was the type you wanted to punch out, but you felt sorry for him, more than hating him.

"Yeah," Jim agreed. "Half the time you wanted to smack him in the puss. The rest of the time you sort of felt sorry for him. This wasn't the place for his type. A few of us are a little bigoted, and maybe one or two are real bigots (Tom was there. He was the type Clint didn't like. There was something wrong with anyone who wasn't of white European ancestry and from Vermont or New Hampshire or wherever he was from. Jim got along with him pretty well, most of the time, but he could grind on anyone's nerves, at times. He was the last one who might glom onto the fact he was the object of the statement.), but most are pretty open. Boquete's got the snobby bigot types, more than here. It's why I avoid the place."

They chatted about various things. Clint had what he could learn from them, so soon excused himself and went on to talk to others. He didn't learn more than that everyone who encountered the five had much the same to say about them. It was fairly obvious that killing Benton had to do with something that had happened somewhere else.

Somewhere at least one of the five was at the time it happened.

Clint walked on down past the super and to the ferry dock. A few people were fishing, and some kids were swimming on the other side of the building, ducking each other and making a lot of happy noise. Two of the Indio children, about nine or ten years old, came running up to hug him and say, "Yantoro! Moga me dende?" ("Greetings! Where are you going?") He played his game with a quarter in one hand and a dime in the other. He put his hands behind his back and passed the coins back and forth, then brought his fists out front for them to slap the hand they wanted. They got the coin in the fist they slapped.

"I'm just walking around, looking for four men and a woman from the states, but born here."

"Ho! The 'blah' people," Tonio said cynically. "They went to Drago on the early bus."

"Blah people?"

"Uh-huh. Totally blah. No sense of humor. Walk around looking at everything, but not seeing anything. Not good and not bad. Paco plays basketball, sometimes. He's not good, but he's not bad."

"Yeah!" Sindro agreed. "He's there because they have to have so many people to make it a game, and not just hoops."

Clint chuckled. "That about describes them!"

He chatted with the kids, who soon went back into the water to join the melee. He strolled on back toward the parque, spoke to several people, then went to the police station. Sergio didn't have anything. A computer check didn't bring up anything, other than their birth dates and school records. They all went to university, no one had excelled at anything. They were average in anything they did, it would seem. Nothing but their pictures in the year-books. Never a mention of them in the school (or any other) paper.

"Really 'blah' people, according to Tonio and Sindro," Clint said, with a grin.

"That describes them to a T," Sergio replied. "I can't picture them doing anything like this."

"Oh, I can!"

"What do you mean?"

"They've held in their emotions for their whole lives. It erupted in a lump."

Sergio shook his head, but agreed that might be a good way to put it. Colorful, but descriptive! "Like when the house was burning, and Old Lady Menendez was locked inside, and little mousey Chico ran up and ripped the door off its hinges. Stuck his hand through that little observation glass, and didn't even get a scratch. Superhuman strength for five seconds from a skinny teenager who never seemed to react much to anything. His brother died in a house fire, six years before, and he was close and helpless. Now it was happening again, but to a stranger. He didn't even remember doing it. Several of the firemen saw it, and couldn't believe it. They were big men, and couldn't have yanked that two inch thick nispero door off the hinges. It took three of them to lift the damned thing after they got the fire out."

"Which means even that mousey little blah woman could have exploded the same way."

"I tend to think whoever did it had a damned good reason, though I don't make more than a personal judgment about that kind of thing. That's for the court to decide."

"It depends on what's behind it. There's something that brought up a lot of hate in one flash. I'm not small, but the machete would have to literally be as sharp as a razor for me to make that kind of a cut."

"You think it was her, then? It was a man who called."

"I don't know which one it was. I imagine two or more could have been there, and somebody felt they would need an alibi. They're acting pretty normal – for them. It could be because they're trying to not be noticed. Nobody would notice them, anyway, so it's hard to say they're acting any different than they always have."

"Nobody would know. Nobody ever paid them any attention. Nothing to compare."

"C'est la vie!"

"Yo tambien."

Clint grinned and went home. He would have to wait until they came back from Boca del Drago to try to get a clue from personality – or whatever.

Chapter three

"I talked to her once. She was at the China, and we were waiting in line together. She seemed a pleasant enough person, in a way. I couldn't get interested in anything she said. It was about going snorkeling or fishing or something. They didn't get anything, the camera's batteries went dead, so they only got a couple out of focus pictures. She talks in a sort of drone."

"Blah."

Judi cocked her head to the side and grinned at Clint. "That describes her to perfection! You *do* come up with something on occasion!"

"Only it was Sindro and Tonio who came up with that."

"The Indios can peg a person accurately within two minutes of looking at them or hearing them talk – even if they can't understand the words."

"I think it was probably a sudden explosion of emotions by someone who kept their emotions bottled for their whole life, to that point. It all came out at once. It's very possible the one who did it won't remember it at all, except having the machete one second and still having it a few seconds later and Benton laying there cut almost in half."

"I've read about that kind of thing. It does happen. What will you do if it's something like that?"

"As Sergio said, that's for the court to decide."

"But will it get to court?"

"Depends."

She nodded and said she couldn't think of anyone in Bocas who deserved something like that more than

Benton, even though you tended to feel sorry for him, most of the time. He couldn't help it if his parents were animals. He was raised to be the same species they were. It was just that you would think anyone would have the intelligence to see they were the misfits, just by the way people reacted to them.

"He just saw it as the way all those chinks and spades and wops and spics always act. The fact he couldn't get along with anyone else never even registered to his, excuse the expression, mind. The world always was out to get the real men and drag them down," Clint said. "It's sad we're talking ill of the dead, but there just isn't anything good to say about him. I'm not the type to suddenly forget the facts about a person. The fact he's dead doesn't change what he was one iota. The fact we can't think of anything good to say about him tells the truth of the story."

"Don't try to be deep. You aren't!"

Clint chuckled and gave her the finger. She laughed.

"Jude, see if your method of gathering information will work enough to find if anyone ever heard any one of them mimic anyone's voice."

"I've been doing that. A couple of people heard one of them telling a bawdy – for them – story that he did a mimic of a gay voice to perfection. Trouble is, they can't remember which one it was. They were all there."

"I'm used to finding one person who's good at blending strictly into the background, but not a group! They'd probably make damned good detec ... hmm. So!" Clint stopped, and looked thoughtful.

"What?"

"I think I just had a thought."

"You think too much. Detectives? All of them? What does that have to ...?"

"Five people who have virtually no past? Five people with an uncanny ability to blend into the background so even a trained very observant person can't remember exactly who said or did what?

"Judi, tell me something about Benton – I mean, besides his act. Nobody could actually be that totally insensitive."

"What do you mean?"

"What do you remember about him, other than that he was an ass. What did he ever do? What did he ever say? Did anyone ever have a real conversation with him that wasn't some kind of wild bigoted rant?"

"I see! You tended to damp him out and think of more pleasant things when he was there. His voice was grating, too. It added to the effect. He was acting. They're all acting. They're damned good at it!"

"Jude, it's your method, greatly refined. You gave them information you came up with without realizing you were doing anything other than make a remark or two to make them think you were listening. You weren't. Lucia was there deliberately to learn what you'd heard about me and Sergio and whatever. What did you tell her?"

"Besides that you didn't have a clue about ... so that was her using my method on me! She's *damned* good at it!"

"And you didn't give her any information. You're used to the method enough that you wouldn't. Automatically.

"I wonder if she's aware of that? If not, we can use it.

"Jude, we tackle this one from another angle. Time to use the airhead act a little – stress *little* – bit with them, Okay?"

She smirked. "So two can play that game. Let's see

who's better at it!"

"And don't forget for one second – if what we suspect about them is true, they're very professional killers."

"Who make slips now and then."

"Such as?"

"The method was bound to get attention. The followup was stupid. All they had to do was nothing, and we wouldn't have glommed onto them. That call to Sergio was just plain stupid."

"I wonder about that. Be careful, Jude. That cut was excessive. There really was a lot of emotion behind it. It was a mistake that was followed by another that was more telling."

She nodded.

They talked awhile about other things. Clint waited until she left to go through all his little traps. He would know if anyone had been in his house looking for anything.

No matter how professional. He knew some tricks, himself. No one had been there. He set another few traps, made sure his comp didn't have anything on it to show he'd been interested in them, put some things on that would indicate that he was looking into something else, or in all the wrong places, then went to the police station. He'd put a little program on the comps several months ago to tell what information anyone was seeking in them, and when. There was only one suspicious entry, but in an area that wouldn't show more than a normal police check on identities.

So. They thought their cover was excellent to perfect.

Be honest! It was excellent, but not perfect. It wouldn't show that he had them figured, past a very minor point. He basically wanted to know what this was about, and whether it was entirely CIA or in conjunction with some other agency. More than one made that likely. More than two made it very scary. It was definitely big. *Very* big!

He went back to the ferry dock. Lando, another Indio kid about ten years old, was there, and ran to hug him and play the game. He got the quarter (Clint had substituted the second quarter behind his back) and ran to buy two icies, one for Clint. They chatted. Clint learned that the blah people actually asked some telling questions of the kids. Questions the kids never suspected were asked or answered. Questions about Benton, Clint, and Judi. Questions about what the police asked them (nothing).

Clint explained that those people were trained to get information in ways you didn't know you'd given any, so be careful.

Lando said he'd warn all the kids. They'd act just like always, but the information would be different. Those half-gringos would learn that they were dealing with people with a lot more smarts than they'd let on. What information did Clint want them to get?

Clint grinned, and told him it might be a good idea to let them know, in very small ways, that the Indio kids had them figured to the nth degree.

"Be sure they know it's all of you, and not one or two. They're dangerous people. If it's all of you, they have to find a way that others won't find out. One or two of you, and you might end up like Benton."

"I didn't think about it, but the Benton-grouch was doing the same thing, wasn't he?"

"I think so. I just don't know why. I have to find which organizations sent them here. They are *not* the blah people they want everyone to think they are. Be very extra careful. If you have any doubts whatever, don't be around them at all or at any time."

He nodded, and looked serious a moment, then grinned. "So the street urchins figured them. They don't give a shit, and won't say anything if maybe they get a nice little handout, now and again. Say a whole dollar instead of a dime."

Clint grinned and ruffled his hair. He hugged Clint, and went on his way. Those kids were more savvy than he was! They were already suspicious, and would have figured it by themselves soon. Maybe it was good that Clint would have them let out that every damned one of them had the same thing figured. It wouldn't do a bit of good to try to shut them up, and shutting up one or two would lead to disaster.

Clint headed back home, thought, then stopped at the internet café. There might be a thing or two he could learn about this from another angle!

Chapter four

None of them had a registered driver's license anywhere he looked in the records. None of them ever owned a car. Only two had records of ever renting apartments, and that because of deposits on the electricity and water in Macon, Georgia.

Lyle Friendly had a minor traffic ticket for overtime parking in Richmond, Virginia. For a person who didn't ever have a driver's license?

"Richmond, Virginia," also told its own story. Veddy eenter-esdink! There were a few holes in their covers, it seemed.

A check in Alister, Rhode Island, showed that he had a license there. The records showed that he was born at Mercy General in 1982, from the driver's license application. The birth records had been lost in a fire in 1983! Wow!

If he had had the time he would have checked every state. He checked Panamá records, and found he was supposed to have been born in Santiago in, Surprise!, 1982. Panamanian mother, gringo father. That was probably real. Rhode Island was as far as most would check.

Which one did Sergio have? He called. Sergio looked it up and said the Panamanian one – and what was going on?

"A whole lot more than we either one guess. Be very careful that no one knows we know anything more than that they're here and are being looked at superficially because they seemed to have met with Benton a few times." He agreed.

Now. How to find out what the hell this was about. Why a little tourist town in Bocas del Toro, Panamá? That would take some careful and discreet digging.

Clint thought, and called Manny Mathews, a friend living on Isla San Cristobal who was actually Marko Bocinni, a major mafia character who had moved to Panamá to escape his past life and raise a family who wouldn't be embarrassed by how pops made his. He helped Clint in a lot of his cases. He was in a unique position to get information. The word was out that he was living on a private island in the Mediterranean.

He would try to find anything, but wasn't in that end of information. He next called Manolo, an agent for several world police organizations, who was working undercover as a shady dealer in something-or-other. He didn't have any information, though there were some small rumors about agents from England, France, Italy, Germany, et al spotted in Panamá. There always were.

He waited until time for the last bus to return from Drago. They weren't on it. The driver said they had booked one night at the hotel there. Rudolfo, the door boy on the bus, said they had met some bigshot on a yacht in the bay, just inside of the island. They seemed to know each other. People were saying it was Jimmy Buffet's yacht, but he knew that one from before, and it wasn't. He would have come to the marina, like always, not anchored offshore like that.

Clint expected information about those five would be extremely hard to come by. He wasn't disappointed, so far. Not much he could do until they returned. He could figure on some way to get what he wanted when they were there. He called Judi, and they went into town for the evening. Dinner at Nine Degrees, then the usual haunts. He didn't learn anything more.

Clint waved to Judi from his hammock on his deck, just at sunrise. He usually could be found there, watching the display of colors over the water at sunrise. He waved to several friends going by on their way to work or to go out for fish or whatever. Arnie Carmody came to his deck at about six with two girls from France who wanted to go snorkeling and such. Would Clint like to come along? – and why didn't he ever wear anything in the mornings?

Clint didn't put on clothes until he decided what he was going to do for the day. Everyone knew it. The question was rhetorical, and didn't get a response, except the two girls giggled, and one, Annette, said it was refreshing to be in a place where they could be so free. Nicole agreed.

Clint went inside and put on a bathing suit, gathered a few odd things, and joined them. They went out near the Zapatillas and Crawl Cay to spend a few hours relaxing and having a good time. He got back at about 4:45 to find three of his little traps sprung. Someone had been in the house. He called Judy, who explained she had the vigilante meeting, so was gone from one until three. She hadn't seen anything there. The five in question had returned to Bocas Town on the 1:00 bus, so they were around.

Clint checked the e-mail and missed phone calls. Nothing new or different. He'd gotten two unanswered calls from the Hotel Olas number at 1:15 and 1:30. Checking to see if he was home, probably.

He checked the video-recorder, expecting to find

nothing. He found nothing. They would certainly know how to handle that kind of thing.

He cleaned up, shaved, had a cup of coffee, and went into town on his bike. Three of the five were at the Toro Loco, so he parked and went inside to have a Balboa and chat with friends a bit. It was early, and not many were there so he, quite naturally, ended up talking with Lucia Aumond, Lyle Friendly, and James Carter. They were doing the blah routine perfectly. He would have been entirely bored stiff with them in two minutes if he didn't know it was an act. He did catch Friendly giving a short questioning look at Aumond in the mirror. That decided him!

"Oh, yeah, by the way, you don't need to sneak around to find what's on my comp. You can come in and check it out anytime I'm home. I ain't stupid enough to have anything that means anything on it, so it's mostly a silly waste of your time," he said, conversationally. That got a shocked look from Aumond and a laugh from Friendly.

"How did you figure us?" he asked. "We didn't think anyone would be able to connect the dots with us. It's important that we know what to avoid."

"Nobody is as totally, as the Indio kids said, blah, as the bunch of you. They're the ones who originally tumbled. They're about ten times as sharp as people give them credit for being."

He laughed again. The others just seemed very nervous.

"What do you think it's about?" The question was one of interest, but casual.

"Oh, I don't really give a hot diddly-damn," Clint replied. "It gets out of hand when somebody gets killed. That was damned stupid, and 'way past professional.

"I do know how he could make you want to smack him one, but that's a long way from knocking him off. That was one hell of a chop. Does the one who delivered it even remember doing it?"

"No comment!" Carter said sharply.

"Let's say he could send almost anyone into an uncontrollable rage. He must have done that with the wrong person," Lucia replied. "Jim, he knows all about it. He just wants to know what's behind it. He doesn't play games. Fifty people told us that. He's also someone who's pragmatic enough to know when to back off of something dangerous.

"Mr. Faraday, this is about something to do with four governments. None of them like the others. He was playing a stupid game that could have ended up in a little war that would go on and on for years, and resolve nothing."

"You represent different countries? This is a first cooperative operation?"

She got a sharp look and a head shake from Friendly. Clint still could see them in the mirror.

"It's not on that order. We're trying to see it doesn't get to that stage."

Carter nodded his approval. Also in the mirror. They apparently didn't know about Clint's exceptional peripheral vision. He wasn't looking at the mirror at any time. He was looking at Lucia when she spoke. She was a bit to the side of where he could see the mirror directly with normal vision.

Clint chatted a bit more, then said he had a date, and left. He had a bit of what he needed. Benton was a side trip. Killing him had to do with something other than their assignment. There was a lot of personal hatred in the way he was killed.

He went to the Golden Grill. The D'Angelo brothers were there, and casually glanced as he passed. They seemed disinterested in him and everything else to the point of total boredom, but Clint saw the watchful look in Paco's eyes.

They didn't look like brothers. He doubted they were. They may be close cousins, but the usual family features simply weren't there. Tony looked Italian, while Paco looked something else. There were features that reminded him of Machian Armachev, a Latvian man in Panamá City. More like his Man Friday, from Turkey or ... Macedonia! The nose and eyes. The skin tone. It was all there. Possibly Slavic. That area of Europe.

He was going to have to find out a lot more about that group. It was going to take a lot of digging in the hardest places. He had to know what the connection was, and with whom. If they'd level with him, he'd probably forget it and go fishing. The way they were handling it, he would go into them as deeply as he could.

He was not going back to the states to find anything. He'd had enough of that. All he'd get was a stone wall with a titanium steel one behind it. He did think maybe he had a clue. It would start with Paco D'Angelo.

He had stopped by the counter. Celia brought him out of thought with, "Clint? What's the matter? You look like you're in some other world, all of a sudden."

"I was trying to remember something. It's one of those things where you know the answer as well as you know your own name, you just can't think of it. A senior moment!

"Café negro and some hojaldres."

"No hojaldres. Empanada or tortillas."

"Cheese empanadas. Two."

He went to the table beside the D'Angelos and sat. They seemed very relaxed, in a wary way. When he knew, he could see the watchful signs. The foot around the chair leg. The occasional darting of the eyes when someone came in or passed very close.

He felt evil. When Celia brought his order, he told her to bring two cold Balboas to the two gentlemen at the next table. They heard him, and tensed, but seemed not to notice to anyone not aware of what they were. When Celia brought them the beers, they managed to look surprised, and to hold them up and say, "Mil gracias!" Clint waved halfheartedly and looked away, using that peripheral vision. They slightly shrugged at each other. Tony took out a cell phone and sent some kind of text message. He held the phone under the table edge a bit where no one could see it – he thought. About a minute later the phone vibrated enough for Clint to hear the buzz. Tony looked at the return text message and grinned at Paco. He came over and said, "Well, Faraday! Having a little fun with us?"

Clint grinned at him, and said, "To tell the truth ... yup!"

He laughed. "How did you tumble to us?" Clint waved at the other chair, and for Paco to come over. He came, and brought Tony his beer.

"Before I ever laid eyes on you people were telling me how there were five people here who were so blah you got bored if you were in the same room. One or two in five, maybe. All five? Huh-uh!"

He laughed. "That's a good thing to know. I guess five people, all of us so damned dull we couldn't cut hot butter, would be beyond belief."

"Too much of the same teacher," Clint agreed. "Lucia's sort of goodlooking and could dress to show off a really good figure, instead of hiding it. She should be more gregarious, and just a bit sensitive and reserved. An attitude of 'I've been hurt enough with a line!' kind of thing. Paco should be more a brooder. You could do the strikeout gigolo bit. Carter and Friendly could be the bore-you-to-tears type. Benton played his act ... to ... perfection." Clint saw something drop solidly into place then. He looked over Paco's shoulder toward the street to cover that. He was looking at a dark, well-dressed man who was passing. The two turned to look.

"Sorry," Clint said. "Someone just went by who I didn't ... it's business."

"You have business with Ahmad? He didn't say he knew anyone here," Paco said. Tony was wide-eyed. That was a slip that should *not* have been made! That Ahmad wasn't supposed to know them was why he was passing, and not coming in. Clint remembered the old country song, "Just walk on by, wait on the corner...." about knowing someone you weren't supposed to know. How? Why?

He remembered they had met with someone with a yacht at Drago.

"Ahmad? I was looking at the heavy man over by the parque. Bill. He owes a lot of people a lot of money. He cons them. He's taken it too far.

"So. Who's Ahmad?"

"A man who has far too much money. We saw him in Boca del Drago, and asked about him," Tony covered. "It seems a lot of people are scared of him. You're aware of a little of why we're here. We want to know why he's here. It seems an unlikely place for such as him."

"It's unlikely for the bunch of you," Clint replied. "Panamá gets a hell of a lot more than its share of silly little intrigues. We're not used to the bigger things, but we have some practice. A few of us. I'd think your CIA contacts would warn you about it."

"We are *not* CIA! Very definitely!" Paco protested.

"Not all of you."

"None of us," Tony said. "We do have some contact with them, but it's not a friendly type. They interfere with little things that soon become big things, heading in another direction." Aumond, Friendly, and Carter came in as they were saying this. They came up behind Tony as Clint said, "That's the object."

"Yes, except they're so damned incompetent that it goes off in a direction nobody wanted," Carter replied.

Clint nodded agreement. "Not a few of them are worse than what they're supposed to be fighting."

"It's a fucked-up world!" Paco said sadly. "I think it would get better very fast if all of us would just go home and say, 'Screw it!' Things start out slow and calm, then get nasty, mostly because the wrong person is used for the wrong job."

"Case in point. Benton."

"Amen!" Friendly said.

They chatted for a little while. Clint didn't learn a lot – but he knew he was looking in the wrong place for answers with that bunch. He should be concentrating on someone else.

He excused himself and went home to use the computer, thought better of it, and went to Ben Longstreet's house.

Ben had been a close friend since he moved to Bocas Town. No one would consider checking his computer.

Clint asked some questions in several places.

About Benton.

Chapter five

Benton had a more complete record. He was actually born in Joplin, Missouri, 1963, and raised in Mississippi, 1971-73, and Missouri, 73-1981, with some stints in northern Louisiana, Texas, and Arkansas. His father was a trucker with the seniority to move to where the better jobs were. His mother was a seamstress. Both drank too much, at times, but not often. Everything was normal enough for the type until he went to high school and was in ROTC. He got into some minor trouble, brawling and badass things, but went into the marines when he was eighteen. He was a normal type of recruit for the first year, then the records started getting spotty, and things were deleted and changed. Clint noted the change in pattern. He went to the University of Arkansas, 1985-1987 where he was a good student the first year, then started getting into trouble with the redneck bit and dropped out the second year. There wasn't much more. He'd worked in sketchy places at sketchy jobs. He'd moved to Panamá. Lots of information, then none.

Clint thought for a minute, then went to the university archives and started comparing what he found on the "official" sites to what was in things where people wouldn't bother to look if they had contact with some redneck bigoted asshole, even if they were working for the kinds of organizations this bunch were working for.

He was in all the yearbooks. 1985, 1986, 1987, 1988. He was a better than average student. He studied criminality and social science. He studied psychology. He got a general science degree in 1989. He had a passport since

1989 that was renewed in 1999 and was renewed in 2009. It was sent directly to the consulate at Albrook. Automatic renewal.

So. He was an educated man with a degree who had dropped out the second year because he was an extreme redneck. He then disappeared for twenty years, for all practical purposes, until he moved to Panamá in 2009. His passport was automatic renewal, which told Clint one hell of a lot more than anyone in those organizations he worked for wanted said. He died in Panamá in 2011.

Clint checked worldwide data through secondary and less sites. Benton had been stationed in much of the world when he was in the marines. He had worked for the US Embassies in Yemen, Saudi Arabia, Monrovia, Gibralter, France, Italy, Romania, Libya et al – as a chauffeur or security guard. His passport was, naturally, always diplomatic. His newest wasn't diplomatic – but was with automatic renewal?

It was stamped every year since he was in the marines, except 1985 and 1986.

A redneck asshole brawler with an education who worked with the American Embassies all those years. Uh-huh. So. He was a CIA operative, a much higher-up one, who was living in Bocas del Toro, Panamá, for two years as a retiree who couldn't speak one sentence in passable English, though he had a college degree.

Clint checked on the aunt who had died and left him property through the registro. His aunt's name was, apparently, Linda Peria V. de Perlas, a Panamanian widow, 92 years old, living in Brunswick, New Jersey, since 1981 when her husband of thirty one years died..

She moved to the states in 1991, and kept the house, that

had been lived in the whole time, in Bocas Town?

He checked the records. She had a permit to rent the place. The tenants were removed when she died.

So. The spinster aunt's husband died ... this was a stupid mess! Whatever precipitated it happened too fast for the records to be changed completely. Those records were for the general public's use. This group obviously knew better.

So why bother, at all?

Okay. Last year the group came for, apparently, the first time. It was thrown together to give Benton a little time to establish something. Clint knew all he had to know about him, now. All he needed, and not of much importance, was why he was used here.

Clint knew Benton spoke poor to fair Spanish. He worked in all those embassies from as little as two months to as much as nine. He probably spoke ... back to the school records.

He took Chinese, French, Spanish, in college. His grades were excellent, in those classes. In the 1989 yearbook he was noted as "The most versatile interpreter of the decade." He had an ability with many languages. German, English, Chinese, French, Slavic, Arabian, and Greek were listed. That was the only distinction he earned the whole four years.

He was used because he had that talent. He probably could listen and know precisely what was being said almost anywhere, while acting like he didn't know more than "Hello" in any of the places.

What could be that big here? Was he here because he spoke Spanish, or because he spoke one or more of the other languages in the resume' – and which ones were the important ones?

There was still a lot Clint didn't know. He had to find out about one other. Maybe he could get some answers from that angle. He thought for a few minutes, then thanked Ben and Earl for the use of the computer. Ben would immediately erase all the sites he checked from the registry and history.

Clint went home, ate a snack, noted that it was dark, sighed heavily, and looked at the clock.

Good lord! 1:47! Eight hours on Ben's comp!

He showered and went to bed.

In the morning at first light, Clint took his boat out and went up and around Boca del Drago. The yacht wasn't there. He swore, then reasoned Ahmad had been in Bocas Town last night, so the yacht was probably there. He went on around and through the bay, to find the yacht was moored out from the marina on Isla Carenero. He took the name and noted it was flying a Libyan flag.

He went on by and back to his place. This time, he went to Judi's to use the comp. Maybe they would think to check hers, but he figured they would know he would check out Ahmad from the instant they brought his name up. The fact he acted like he didn't register, they would know better. They would have the information that showed he didn't miss much along those lines. Ever.

His name was (most probably) Ahmad Abdul Museffa, from Syria, living in or near Libya, though the company the yacht was registered to, that he owned the controlling interest in, was international, with its main offices in Cairo and Paris. Branches were listed in more than ten countries. He was an oil broker. He was sixty four years old, and a very hardnosed businessman.

Oil? Why Panamá?

Venezuela, of course. And the canal. And the pipeline. There was talk of making an overland route for carrying huge tankers of oil across Panamá because some of them were simply too big to use the present canal. The idea that they could carry those tankers across on an overland road was ludicrous to Clint – but it was, supposedly, a serious discussion. The fact that most proposed routes meant they would have to climb more than a thousand meters to cross mountains would mean use of more damned fuel than the tanker could carry! His nutty author/musician friend, Dave, had said that there was a plan to use steam and an atomic boiler for motive power. "No atomic energy for power generation, but we'll use a mini-reactor in every truck to haul the fossil fuel that'll have to be used because of our 'no nuclear' rule. Shit for brains!"

Was that what this was about? It didn't seem likely, but you never know. As Dave noted, "Shit for brains!" Clint wouldn't argue that one.

How to connect? How to find what was really going on? Was this another case of money-mad people trying to con a country into something stupid?

Whatever. Clint was curious enough that he'd try to learn what was happening, who, where, and why. He would enjoy this kind of thing, because it would entail finding little things that were purposely and professionally hidden. It was the kind of thing that the computer could make obsolete. If something was done in a panic, something was done in too much of a rush, things would be missed. If they'd had time, the information about Benton wouldn't have been there. Now it was out, and there wasn't much reason to try to hide anything more. There was a definite effort by the US to clamp down on computer use and access, but that would prove to be another idiotic project to attempt. The knowledge was already out there, and too many places were already holding copies of all the information. Clint didn't doubt that fifty sites had already downloaded the information, many of them in foreign and not-at-all friendly countries, that could be used for comparison with later information. Excising Benton from the records was a futile pursuit. Even if the college records and passport records could be expunged now, they had the old records that they would certainly check. The world was about to undergo some tremendous changes. It was occurring – far too late – that the old political tricks and schemes had zero chance of working anymore. All that stuff was recorded when it came out. Changing it later was more a way to call attention to it than to hide it.

Back to the case. Maybe he should get it off his mind for awhile. Maybe he could chat with the blah five a bit more and learn something.

Maybe he just *did* learn something! It occurred to him now, anyhow!

Why were they still here? It would seem getting rid of Benton was a way to stop whatever. They would then leave. The longer they stayed, the more likely connections would be made.

Why the hell was *Ahmed* here at all, much less *still* here?

There was at least one more someone, someone more important than Benton, involved and here. Benton was killed because he could expose that someone, not because of what that someone was up to.

That was really scary. Clint could be in a very bad spot

if he discovered who and/or what. His life wouldn't be worth the old "two cents" the minute he had answers to those two questions.

That meant he'd go after answers a lot more intensely – and one hell of a lot more carefully.

Chapter six

The five were sitting at the Grand Muralla, having breakfast, so Clint went in to join them.

"Learn anything new?" Aumond asked.

"New? About what? Oh – your affairs," Clint answered. "When I have the time. I'm not too interested, unless someone else is killed. The one thing I'll warn you about, something everyone around here knows about me, is not to involve any innocent people with this kind of silly crap. That goes triple for the Indios here, who aren't involved, in any way. They don't know anything, and they couldn't care less about these idiotic intrigues.

"I suppose it's about the oil. That's beyond silly, anyhow. All anyone has to do is think about it for two minutes, and they'll know it's worse than stupid. I don't think anyone can con Panamá into sinking a penny into that fantasy."

Tony laughed. He seemed to be the only one who didn't take it seriously, in the first place. "It has a lot of scientific backing, in most ways. I'd call it science fiction, not fantasy. Seems a lot of science fiction is more prediction. Arthur Clarke, for instance."

"Science fiction – like smoking cigarettes isn't harmful to your health, it's more about genetics? There are a lot of so-called scientists who were in on that crap. Big-deal 'scientists' are in court every day with bullshit 'facts' for the jury. You can buy them a dime a dozen anymore."

He laughed again. "Ain't it the truth? You don't know what to believe. Too many use the net to find information, which means all you have to do is get some, as you say,

'So-called scientist' to distribute phony facts, and they then become real in uninformed people's minds.

"You think that's behind this?" He seemed interested, so it wasn't.

Clint smirked. "I haven't concentrated on it much. Using the net for actual facts isn't hard to do anymore. You just have to know where to find the reality. Most things are kept in numerous places. You have to know where to look for the information that was put there before the so-called 'expunging' of the records was done. It's still there, and can't be removed. You can go back and try to change a lot of it, but that'd mean fifty different sites and some way to enter and edit.

"Forget it! Not gonna happen!"

He was the only one who didn't seem shocked at the statements. Clint grinned at the others, and changed the subject. He'd let them wonder about what he may have found in older records on other sites.

"You know about the Mayan predictions ending the world next year? December or thereabouts?" Paco asked, seriously. "I begin to wonder more and more if maybe there's more to them than we know. Having all that information to hand ... things could get pretty bad for a lot of people."

"For a lot of politicians and dictators," Clint agreed.

"It's frightening! I don't scare easily," Aumond cried, and shuddered.

"It makes your jobs as much as obsolete," Clint agreed. "I'd never checked on Benton before. There wasn't any reason to that I knew about. It took ten minutes to learn he was a language expert with the CIA for more than twenty years."

"So! That was why he was used? He was a language expert?" Carter asked, clearly shaken. "What languages? Did you learn that?

"I'd like to know how you found that kind of information. Our organizations only knew he was mixed up in various things in various places where information was lost or intercepted in ways we didn't know. It was connected to him, but we didn't know how. All we knew was that he would go to a place, and suddenly the CIA knew far too much about our ... projects."

"I'd think you could have figured it long ago," Clint replied. "What the hell did you think was happening?"

"We thought he had some way to get locals or our own people to give him information."

"If I recall the information, he spoke French, German, Greek, Italian, Libyan, Spanish, Arabian, Monrovian, and several more in college."

"Christ! He never finished college! He dropped out after two years, and knew all that?" Friendly cried.

"He finished four years, and had a degree in what amounts to political science," Clint said. "He was known as the best interpreter of the decade at the University of Arkansas. Don't try to tell me your organizations missed that! The bit about dropping out and as much as disappearing from the scene was the cover. He worked at embassies from when he was in the marines until two years ago, when he came here when he inherited that place from his Panamanian spinster aunt who had moved to New Jersey when her husband of thirty years died. She had the place here rented out until he supposedly inherited it and moved in. That didn't take half an hour to find! It's a standard by-the-book cover tale!"

"How do you find them? Which sites? Why didn't anyone in any of them ... why weren't those sites checked?" Carter demanded. "None of our, er, sponsors, checked what you found in half an hour? *Why, damn it!*?"

"The university archives have copies of all the yearbooks. He went to the University of Arkansas for four years. He was in all the yearbooks for those four years," Clint said condescendingly. "I would think that kind of thing would be checked, first thing. I can't picture any savvy organization in the business you're in not checking that kind of thing as routine."

"You'd think they could think," Aumond snarled acidly. "Apparently, that's not a prerequisite to the job. After all, it could get us all killed, not *them*!"

"We're surrounded by incompetents, but that's just par for the course. 'It's good enough for government work' is true a hell of a lot of the time," Friendly snarled. "You know, I think maybe the Mayans are right. They didn't say the world would end, only that it would go through catastrophic change. With what's happening in the world, they have the timing about right."

"C'est la vie! I'd better get going. I just came into town for some groceries," Clint said. "I'd advise you that a lot of your 'solid' information's not too accurate, and to be very careful. You're dealing with people like you."

Tony really laughed at that.

Clint went on to the China and home with the groceries. He called Sergio with his throwaway phone and told him much of what had been said and done, and about Benton.

"I figured. Some idiot from the US consulate came and told me they would investigate it, because he was an American citizen, and may have been involved with drug smuggling or some such crap."

"To which you replied?"

"It is a murder. It is in Bocas Town, Isla Colón, Bocas del Toro, Panamá. *I* am in charge of investigating violent crimes. I would appreciate his cooperation in my investigation. I would *not* turn it over to some stupid foreign agency I've learned through sad experience not to trust one millimeter to pursue."

"To which he replied?"

"Blah, blah, blippety blah."

"Typical."

"Uh-huh. You found out one hell of a lot that we couldn't find. I'd like to learn your method."

"Go to old records on the net. The newer ones are, shall we say, altered."

"Yes. The problem is that I don't know which older records to check."

"Whatever occurs to you when you sit in front of the screen. On most subjects, you can rely on what's current in a lot of cases. On things like this, you have to find the records made before the alterations began." They talked awhile more, then Clint rang off, and decided to see if he could find anything more about the proposed new project to move the oil tanker overland. He wanted to know what Ahmad's connection was. That might mean finding a lot of facts about him.

An hour later, he knew little more. This was a case of a man who seemed to be in the spotlight quite often in mostly unimportant ways for so-so reasons. His companies were in a lot of different places, and dealt with a lot of different things. Mostly to do with oil production and distribution. He had a lot of power that he used judiciously. He made about two million per year, if the records could be believed. He gave away about that much to various causes and charities.

Bullshit! That 230 foot floating palace cost him more than fifteen million! What was inside probably cost as much or more. He was known for collecting antique jewelry, and had paid more than three million dollars for some old emerald tiara worn by some long-dead empress. He had quite a lot of things from the Americas with historical value. He had bought numerous items from the pirate cache Clint found four years ago. He had gone to Panamá City for the first time to bid on the treasure. He went through the canal, and was impressed. He came back to Panamá a couple of times since, once in April, 2009.

Okay. Whatever, it had come about in the past couple of years.

Two or maybe a little longer. Benton had been in Bocas for that long. He was sent in too much of a hurry, so it was something that had happened fairly fast. He arrived in Bocas in early May, 2009. That timing had to mean something. That, plus the fact they hadn't enough time to get the records in place to explain him. Something happened in late March or early April of 2009 that Clint would have to concentrate on. He also wanted to know, for his own edification, why the five were still here. That "why" had to do with a "who" – and it wasn't Ahmad. He was here for the same reason they were here.

Clint sighed. He would have to go to Panamá City for answers. He didn't like cities.

Clint took a flight. He wasn't up to a nine hour bus ride, at the moment. He arrived in the city at two thirty, and checked into the Hotel California. He walked around a bit, then went to the police station for more information. He had worked on several cases in the city, and they knew him well. They respected him and the fact he wasn't a glory-seeking pain-in-the-ass violence freak, like in the American novels.

Emilio Barca was the new head of homicide. He'd met him twice before, and was impressed with his professionalism. He would cooperate in any way he could. Clint explained that he was working on an odd murder case in Bocas that had connections to several other countries. Benton was CIA, which the US wanted kept quiet. He also explained that the CIA wasn't aware he was on the case, or that he knew that's what Benton was doing there.

He spent the afternoon looking through any information they had on when Ahmad was there. He had paid for extra security in the city, using off-duty police. They refused to allow him armed guards he brought with him.

Clint talked with two of the officers who were in the city on rotation (Panamá rotates the police every so often. It makes for less corruption if they don't get too cozy with certain people in a given place) and had been paid, very well, for the approved security duty with Ahmad. They said he wasn't the best employer, but he wasn't at all bad. It was just that he seemed to think he was some kind of king or something who could order them around or to do things that weren't legal here. They weren't about to walk into a restaurant and order people at a table he wanted to move!

They didn't know many of the people he met with, but he went to a big plush office by the causeway. Some kind of engineering firm. A lot of Chinese people and some other assorted foreigners. Scientific Solutions Innovators Worldwide, S.A. The guards had to wait in the lobby when he was there. They weren't allowed to go inside to the offices. The elevator always took him to the 22$^{nd}$ floor, the penthouse suites. There was a helipad on top. They knew that, because he had once gone in one for four hours. Hours they had to stay in the lobby to wait for him. At four bucks an hour, they would wait weeks, if he wanted.

Oscar said he saw a man there, maybe a gringo, who Ahmad met in the fancy club outside of town in the ritzy section. He believed he was called Ralph or Rolf.

Clint went to a good restaurant, which Panamá has a number of, then to the hotel for the night. Tomorrow he was going to have to find out a thing or two about SSIWSA.


It was raining in the morning. Clint took a taxi to the SSIWSA building, and went inside. He went to the receptionists counter and asked to speak with someone there, he didn't have a name, except Ralph or Rolf, to do with the oil tanker project. She said she wasn't aware of any oil tanker project, but he may mean Rolf Samson. He didn't work there, but was there a lot of the time to meet with clients to explain investments or research projects. He worked mostly with Mr. Chan and Mr. Moto.

Chan was Chinese, while Moto was Japanese. Neither was on premises today, and wouldn't be until next Wednesday. They were at a meeting in Mexico City. Samson had an office in the Edificio Whitehall. Clint had seen that one, so thanked her and went outside to hail a cab to take him almost across town to the Whitehall

Building. He found the Inversiones Samson Panamá offices, and went up. The secretary said Samson would be in at two. Clint picked up some pamphlets and said he'd be back then. He went back to the hotel and looked over the pamphlets, which were mostly land sales brochures. One was about purchasing land for future projects.

Clint sat back to think. Any of the proposed routes for that silly overland route went through the comarcas. There was no way the Indios would sit back and let the government take anymore of their land. The one scheme Clint held against Martinelli had to do with what seemed a thinly disguised attempt to dispossess Indios of their property in the name of progressive land titling. So far, the Indios were holding their own, and the president didn't need the negative publicity over the rest of the world about it.

He studied the brochures about land acquisition. It was pretty well set that this was purchase of land from the Pacific to the Caribbean in a given area. It was something you wouldn't notice, unless you were looking for that specific kind of thing. He noted very carefully which part of the comarca was on the end of the route. He had been there once before, and knew some of the people in charge in the comarca. He might go there before he returned to Bocas. He got a good lunch in the chicken place two blocks from the Hotel California and headed for Rolf's offices at ten 'til two. He was there and waiting when Samson came in at two ten. Rolf came in the front door, saw him sitting there, and greeted, "Clint Faraday? I'm Rolf Samson. Come on in and we can talk."

He hadn't spoken to the secretary at all. He wanted Clint to be impressed that he would have any information about him, so Clint paid no attention to it and followed him into the plush offices.

"Some people who work for an acquaintance in Bocas said to expect you. What can I do for you?"

"Actually, you just did," Clint answered. "I wanted to know if you were connected to them. You are."

He grinned. "I think I like your cool. I played the trump card, and you finessed it beautifully!"

"I begin to see what this is about. Leave the Indigenos out of your schemes. Only screw the ones who can afford it. I'll stay out of it, to that point."

"The Indios aren't involved. I promise you that."

"Your routes – any of them – go through the comarcas. The Indios won't allow it, so they'll be attacked by the government on some pretense, and dispossessed. It ain't gonna happen if I have anything to say about it."

He studied Clint for a minute, sighed, and said, "You figured this a lot better than I thought. I still say the Indios aren't going to be affected. Trust me."

"Oh? Who? Ahmad?"

He grinned. "No comment!"

"Yeah. He only makes a couple of million a year," Clint said, with his grin. "I don't see how you can make anything on it."

"There were about three zeroes left out of the official financial report. Printer's error."

"Benton's dead. That's a bit too far."

"Benton had nothing to do with my part. There are four distinct parts to this puzzle. The closest to hand was behind that fiasco. It wasn't even their representative who killed him. It wasn't about this, either. It was because of something that happened somewhere and somewhen else that Benton caused. He caused it by turning on the very ones he was supposed to be protecting. Somebody's brother died, as a result."

Clint thought about that. "Friendly's the only one big enough to have done that, except in an insane rage."

"Very true, but rage was part of it.

"Listen, Clint. I wouldn't be a part of this if it weren't about some things that were done to a lot of innocent people to allow Ahmad to get that much money. He's a devil with an angel's facade. I want to get it back. I only want what it'll cost me.

"Panamá can be a very strange place, the way it affects your outlook on life. I'll do things I never would have considered, in other circumstances. It's a matter of looking for the real source of things. In the states, that wasn't easy. It isn't even possible, in most circumstances. There, nobody's exposed to the truth of a lot of things."

"There, I agree. I'll check a bit on what reason Friendly might have for the killing of Benton, and maybe drop it, but that doesn't include staying out of it if my friends or Panamanians get drawn into something nasty."

Samson nodded. They chatted about little inconsequentialities for a little while. Clint found Samson was the kind of person he could be friend's with. They shared a certain philosophy about pragmatism. Panamá affected a lot of people that way.

Still, he wasn't sure he could trust Samson too far. He could be running a con on Clint Faraday, as well as on others. He would have to go slowly and cautiously.

He was going to do one thing, certainly. He wanted to visit his Indio friends in a certain part of a certain comarca.

Chapter seven

Clint greeted Nacio and Keno with hugs. He was welcomed with the usual Indio enthusiasm as he got off the bus. It was a beautiful day, and this was in the lush rain forest area near the coast.

"How is Nita? Samuel?" Clint asked Nacio. Nita was his wife, and Samuel was his six year old son. He said they were doing fine. It was a very good year for crops and cattle. The puebla now had dependable electricity, which was good for television and refrigerators. Keno said he preferred firelight, but you had to go along with whatever passed for progress among the gringos and Latinas. They didn't have the brains to look around to see who was content and who was always looking for things they couldn't have. "They lie and steal and work their butts off to get a thing, then it's not what they wanted from the first."

Clint laughed and agreed that's just the way of the so-called civilized world. Progress that leaves everyone further behind.

After a couple of hours of visiting and meeting with all his friends, he brought up the planned project to put a highway for gigantic tankers from the Pacific to the Caribbean. Their part of the comarca was the only place nearly flat enough for that kind of stupid route.

"No. It would have to be in the mountains," Miguel said. "The land on the flat part has nothing under it but sand and too much water. Even the footpaths that have been there for many centuries have to have new rocks put in every year. The old ones sink when there is a lot of rain in the mountains. The water flows under and the sand gets wet enough that you sink if you try to walk on it. The rocks all sink. You can see that now. It's not even the wet season, and you sink over your boots if you don't stay on the rocks. Even the rocks sink. You cannot get enough rocks to come up from the bottom. For all my life and the lives of my grandfathers and great-grandfathers we have put new rocks in every year, and they still sink, just not as fast as where there are no rocks."

Clint looked thoughtful, then asked if there was any PVC pipe around. Long sections.

They had hundreds of feet of PVC. Clint said it was too flexible for what he wanted.

"You want to see how deep the sand is. It will do it. You will see!" Keno said. "Come! We will waste a few lengths of the government's plastic pipe!"

"How far does the soft part extend out there?" Clint asked.

"How far? Oh! You mean is there a way around it," Miguel replied. "I got used to the way city people talk at University.

"This whole valley, from the mountains to the north until the mountains to the south. Probably two and a half kilometers, and all the way from the trees to the west to past the pass where there are trees to the east. Six or seven kilometers. Our village is in the hills where the ground is solid, and the other is in the hills to the south. There is nothing in the valley, and only the one path that is only used when there is need to move things without going to the road and back on the other side. It is for visiting and emergencies. We do not carry very much, because you will sink, and it is very difficult to go any distance if you are too heavy."

Three men and seven children went out into the mucky field nearby with a rock and mud path across it carrying several twenty foot lengths of 3/4" PVC, off into the muck (where they sank almost to their knees more than a few feet from the path) and started twisting a length of the pipe into the mud. Just pushing and twisting by hand made it sink with little resistance. They attached a second piece, and it went in, going even faster.

"It is below the top crust of harder and drier sand," Miguel lectured. "It will now go very quickly. This top part is floating, because of the pressure of the water from much higher lifting it. You will see."

They pushed two more lengths in, and were starting on a third when Clint said to just pull it all back out. That was more than eighty feet, and it would go in as fast as they pushed it with no resistance to speak of, so it was a huge underground lake. Like Mexico City. The water was probably fairly pure, down there. If they did massive pumping, the whole area would start sinking.

They pulled the pipe back out and went back to the puebla, a happy bunch sharing a joke. Clint played and teased the children, they kicked a soccer ball around a bit, then he had to go. He said he hated to leave – and meant it! He hugged everyone, and promised to return. They knew they were welcome in his home in Bocas, anytime.

He was thinking as he rode the bus back toward the main road. He decided to go back to Panamá City to see if he could find the exact route under discussion. Rolf would probably cooperate.

This was rich! A couple of Indios and some government PVC pipe proved the idea was totally unworkable! A project several dozens of top engineers worked on over a period of some years (the project was first proposed in 1994) was shot out of the saddle by some Indios and some PVC pipe! Clint couldn't stop himself from giggling like a fool, at times. Ten million dollars for those experts and equipment wasted, when all it took was six dollars worth of plastic, and an hour to push it into the muck.

"Greetings! I had to come back to see if you could show me the route the engineers suggested for the road."

Rolf looked a question, and showed some curiosity in it.

"I had some experts and equipment to check on a piece that seems to me to be the only place in the whole schmeer where a flat road could go. We both know how moving that much size and weight over mountains is beyond ridiculous."

"Six or eight different firms have used fifty or sixty engineers and even satellite views to prove the route would be feasible, and would work. They just didn't have a way to figure the ultimate cost," he replied. "I doubt your engineers could add anything important to it.

"Who? That German-Danish group who say the problem would be getting the equipment to do the work into the particular area is as much as using it would cost, thus doubling the cost?"

"Nope! A wad of Indio children!"

"I was told you went up to the comarca. You're not seriously going to say a bunch of Indios proved the world's top engineers are wrong?

"I mean, they probably are, in some details, but not enough to stop the project that won't happen anyway."

"Do they plan to make a floating bridge seven kilometers

long in those engineering plans?"

Rolf let a big grin escape. "So. You've proven what the Indios say is true, and what the engineers say is bullshit?"

"Engineers who had soundings of the close area and a few high resolution pictures from the satellites. Ten minutes going out there and making the simplest tests would have ended this silly fiasco before it started. I guess none of them wanted to get their fancy shoes wet, and they would have had to walk almost a whole kilometer through muck. Not in the job description.

"Hell! If a surveyor had gone out there, he wouldn't have been able to set up his tripods! They would've slowly sunk into the mud, with those pointed legs! The guy holding the stick couldn't be focused on, because he would be sinking, if he wasn't on the path. Maybe on it, in places. That whole valley's like Mexico City. Floating on a lake. Mexico City has a more solid base than there is out there. The satellites didn't show any trees, because there aren't any. In a rain forest area, there aren't any trees? Really?"

"They felt it was solid hardpan."

"With that marsh grass covering it? A hardpan would have made it a shallow lake."

"How deep did you test? Accurate?"

"We only used four lengths of PVC. Eighty feet. Nothing solid or semi-solid past a layer of maybe eight or ten feet of what was peat or something that allowed the sand and muck to build on top. It was just water, after thirty four or five feet. I could read the soundings to see how deep it is. Probably a couple of hundred feet."

He roared with laughter. There were tears rolling down his face from it. "We spent four million dollars for engineers, and you spent four dollars for some Indio kids – and the four dollars was for the bus to get there! I *love* it!"

"Actually, six fifty. I bought sodas and cookies for the kids."

He finally stopped laughing enough to say, "Clint, don't let a hint out that might reach Ahmad, Okay?"

Clint nodded, and said he had to get back to Bocas. "Oh! I meant to ask! Why are they still in Bocas? Why is Ahmad?"

"I wonder about that, myself. It doesn't seem logical, now that they're rid of Benton. I don't know."

"There's someone else pulling strings, somewhere. Be careful!" Clint warned.

Chapter eight

Clint got back to Bocas Town just at dark. He got off the water taxi, and was just getting to the road when he saw Lyle Friendly's back as he stepped out of the Lemon Grass and headed toward the ferry dock.

Clint went upstairs and asked if he was there.

"Friendly? That gringo who doesn't talk to any other people?" Serena asked. "He sits on the deck all the time and drinks Coke. He just left."

Clint went to the deck. From the little table there, he could see the water taxi approach very clearly.

He went on home to check everything out. No one had sprung any traps, but they would know that it would be useless to try to find anything there. He'd made that clear enough!

Friendly was sitting in the Lemon Grass to be where he could see the water taxis come in. They would know he hadn't taken his boat, so would probably come in by water taxi or plane.

It was time to find out who they each were working for. Oil and Rolf's statement about being the closest one meant, most likely, Venezuela, for Friendly. Mexico was probably out of it. They could easily deliver oil to either coast – then again! Maybe they wanted a poker in the fire.

The remarks about Benton knowing too much about their organizations meant ... Syria? That was mentioned. Syria and Libya.

He didn't have enough. He went to the police station and asked Sergio to find what other countries were on the fives' passports. He had checked on them, and should know.

"The US, all of them. Mexico, Saudi Arabia, and Venezuela, Friendly (he had that one right!). The D'Angelos, Italy, Yemen, Iran, France, Australia, Canada, Brazil, here. Aumond, Canada, England, Hong Kong, Romania, Poland, Israel, here. Carter, Mexico, Venezuela, Afghanistan, South Korea, Thailand, and Vietnam," he said after a few minutes for getting the files.

Okay. Working assumption: Friendly, Mexico and Venezuela: D'Angelos, Iran: Aumond, Israel: Carter, Mexico – which meant Friendly was only Venezuela. Probably. How did Ahmad fit this collection? Where? How? Other than being someone who was being suckered into spending a few hundred million on a scam, he didn't quite fit anywhere. Clint wished he'd had a closer look at him, but what he saw definitely didn't look like mid-sixties. He looked mid-forties, from a distance.

Clint called Sergio back into the room and asked about Ahmad Abdul Musefa. There was no one using that passport here. The one on the yacht? Ali Marefalla. He was a president of some kind of engineering company owned by Ahmad.

Clint grinned to himself. The scammers were being conned! Big time! Ahmad was playing them against each other! He called Rolf, after a few minutes thinking. He wasn't at all sure Rolf had been straight with him, but would give him a certain benefit of the doubt.

"Want some news that'll make you laugh out of one side of your face and cry out of the other?"

"What? This has to be good, if you're calling me. Friendly and Aumond meet you when you got back? I didn't think you'd mind if I told them you were coming."

"He'd been watching the water taxis, and she was watching the airport. I should have come over in Paul's boat with him and gone directly to my dock.

"Ahmad isn't Ahmad."

There was a long growing silence.

"You still there, or did you faint?"

"I ain't much the fainting type. Who's there who's supposed to be Ahmad?"

"Ali Marefalla. An engineer. Was he the same one who came here for you to set this up?"

"Uh-huh. An engineer. He probably went out there and found what you found, and decided to use it. He was the one who suggested we fund the project and rake off a few billion in the next ten years."

"He was going to put a hundred million or so up front?"

"You know the routine. He puts up ten million, which is nothing to him, we each come up with ten million. Venezuela, Mexico, Saudi Arabia, Yemen, Brazil, Iran, North Korea, four or five more. I have to check. I'll as much as bet Ahmad controls the dispersion of funds. He'd take all of us for ten million apiece. How do we work him?"

"Why, I'm going to figure it out. He'll know fairly soon that I checked on Ahmad. I'll cut myself in."

"Careful! You'll get cut, but not *in*!"

"How many of you have already put up funds?"

"We have ninety four million in the account, right now. It's offshore, here."

"Let me think about it. I may have an angle they haven't ever considered."

"Such as?"

"To have an account like that you must have a

Panamanian in the corporation, if just in name."

"I'm Panamanian. I was born in Penonomé. Pops was English, and made a quick getaway when I was less than a year old."

"Then we have to show that Ahmad isn't the one who set the account up. He can't have control, if his part was done by proxy. That means that the Panamanian members of the board control the account until he makes a declaration, which will take someone like him a day or less. You'll have about six hours to do something."

"Like get a Panamanian who isn't involved in the business deals to secure the funds until it's resolved? I think that's the way we can handle it, legally. The only problem will be in getting a Panamanian we can trust that much. Too bad you're a gringo."

"I'm Panamanian. Declared and decreed by Basilio Rangero Bonitas, chief of the comarca at Cusapín, and the chief at Rambala. I even have a passport that says I'm Panamanian."

"I heard they can do that. Some doctor was declared Ngobe, the government fought it, and lost. Big time! I'll have a Cessna at the Bocas airport for you at six in the morning. I'll be the pilot. We'll go directly to the islands with the proof you'll supply that Ahmad wasn't Ahmad, and may be running some kind of game.

"You will have the proof?"

"Did Ali sign anything with Ahmad's name?"

"Everything. He probably has a PA."

"That would work – if he told you in writing that he was there with that PA to represent Ahmad. If you weren't so informed, the PA is a piece of paper that you can use to wipe your ass."

"See you at six."

Clint hung up and grinned. He called Sergio and asked that he very quietly get copies of the entry papers for Ali. He could come pick them up anytime he liked.

"Half an hour."

Chapter nine

"Mr. Faraday, I'll have to check with Panamá City before I can do anything with this. I can freeze the transfer of funds, but that's all."

"Horse manure!" Rolf snarled. "I'm in charge of this end, as it says in those contracts right there, and am *not* about to let some lousy crook scam these people out of their money – even if they probably every one deserve it. I've shown you the contracts for these people's funds were garnered through misrepresentation by a person not the one who signed the name of Ahmad Abdul Musefka. If this bank enters into complicity with that crook, I'll see that there's not one person in this world who doesn't know you did so!

"If I wanted the money in my name, I'd expect a very intense investigation. I don't. I want it in the name of a person whose reputation is very clear, and very positive. A man who is so deeply concerned with stopping this kind of thing that he was made a Panamanian in only the second time in the history of Panamá such a declaration was made. He is Panamanian, and Ngobe! I want this man, whose honesty is declared and proven a thousand times over, to hold these funds and see that those deserving don't lose it."

Sardina made a call, and a lawyer for the bank came in, listened to the story, and said the bank had no choice, under the law, but to transfer the funds to a neutral party. Clinton Forrest Faraday was such a person. Why call him? The law was clear enough that no lawyer was needed, except to get the signatures of interested parties on the form. He was there. The forms were on the desk. Both the legal representative of the funds and the neutral recipient were there. Sign the contracts and forms and go get some lunch. The funds would be in Faraday's account within the hour.

So they did that. They were eating a delicious mariscos mix when Rolf's phone buzzed. He answered and put it on speaker.

"Yes? Rolf here."

"This is Ahmad Musefka."

"What do you want, Ali Marefalla?"

"I am Ahmad's legal representative, and have a full power of attorney to act in his name!"

"You didn't bother to state so or to get an agreement from the others that would allow you to sign contracts with them. You didn't even present the PA to the bank. You signed a false name, in law. I repeat, what do you want?"

He hung up. Rolf grinned and giggled. "I think Ahmad's going to be a bit upset over this one."

"Watch your back!" Clint warned.

"Oh, I will!

"What are you going to do with the money? None of us can legally touch it, now. We timed it just right. A single hour more, and he would have thought of an out of some kind."

"I'll see it returned to everyone, minus my ten percent handling fee. You each get nine million back. The comarca there could use a school and clinic. Ten million donation from Ahmad. Tell him I said thanks."

Rolf grinned, and gave Clint a high five.

Rolf even flew Clint back to Bocas. When they landed,

at four o'clock, the five and Ahmad ran out toward the plane, but the guard made them go back into the terminal. Clint waved, and went toward the private gate. They came running out toward him as Rolf took off for Panamá City. He said he was hungry. They could talk over a snack.

He called Judi. She and Sergio would want to be in this, and would join him at the new Mexican place Gary had opened.

It was almost funny how Clint knew exactly what they wanted to say, but couldn't find a way to start it.

"The money's gone. Ali, here, was running a scam on all of you for Ahmad. Each country will get their money back, minus ten percent. Ahmad and his companies will get out of Panamá and not return. He has two branches he has thirty days to divest himself of. He gets nothing from this but an international reputation that's about what it already was. I'll try to get it spread a little better. That's about it."

Friendly laughed. "It's better than any of them deserve. The way I look at it, you saved them each nine million, up front, and a hundred million, in the long run."

"That's not how it'll be seen by ... back in my sponsor's home," Carter said. "They have a different slant on things."

"They would rather have Ahmad con them out of a hundred million than spend one million to find out what was going on?" Judi asked. "What other slant can you have on this kind of thing? Get real!"

"I think my sponsor won't hold it against you, personally, Faraday," Aumond said. "I can make them see they saved a hell of a lot more than the puny couple of million they put out.

"Present it as, 'I was paid to investigate. I did. It was a scam. You would have lost your asses if we hadn't conned Faraday into finding out what was really going on. If you were in Faraday's shoes, you would keep the whole ten million and tell the bunch of you to stick it up your asses!' point out that Clint doesn't have to return a centavo. They got out of this cheap!"

"That'll work!" Paco said. "It's true, really."

"So I'm the only one here who has no way out. Ahmad will see it as a failure on my part that cost him a billion dollars," Ali said unhappily.

"You knew the rules when you got into the game," Clint said. "Don't expect any sympathy from me!"

"Well, I can disappear in a place not too far from here. Ahmad can send someone for his boat." He got up and walked out.

"Ahmad finds him, he's shark bait," Sergio said. They all nodded.

"Most of you can come out alright," Judi said. "Just keep the shit out of Panamá.

"These tamales are good!

"Oh! I meant to tell you! This Tomas D. Harry guy from the big bad US Gov'mint was looking for you. He said you have a lot to answer for. Benton was a US citizen who got killed because of the inefficiency of the Panamanian police department, and he was going to bring it up in congress that blah, blah, blah."

"He tried it on me," Sergio said. "He'd just come from talking to you, and said you were an airheaded bimbo bitch who had her come-upance on overdue, and he was going to see that there were consequences for your attitude."

"What did you do?" Aumond asked. "We met him. He was the typical big bad government O-ficial who was going to see that no one got away with obstructing him and his mission.

"I told him his new mission was to kiss my ass. I'd let him do it for a hundred dollars."

"I asked him for his passport. It said his name was Benjamin Franklin Washington. I said he just filed a report under the name of Harry. He said, 'Oh yeah. Wrong one! Here!' and handed me another," Sergio said, with a chuckle. "He's sitting in a cell while I personally investigate why he has two passports under different names."

"Oh? You're investigating things, personally?" Friendly asked, grinning.

"When I get around to it. Maybe tomorrow or next day."

They joked for awhile, then Clint went home. He needed a shower and a long rest!

Clint was relaxing, watching the sunrise from his hammock on his deck. It wasn't very colorful today, but was somehow rather calming – as if he needed calming!

His phone buzzed. It was Rolf.

"Want an update? Something even you, with all your experience here, won't believe."

"I can't picture what it would be. What?"

"There's a man from France, an engineering firm, who wants investors on a land route for carrying tankers too big to use the canal from coast to coast."

"You, of course, said you'd investigate it and find investors, if it was a good deal."

"No. I said I'd heard the story before. No go."

"Ah! Then he said you could make a deal that was perfectly safe, where you'd make a bundle."

"Something like that."

"And?"

"Guess which company?"

"Ahmad subdivision f, for France, two thousand twenty three!"

"Nope!"

"Okay. Who?"

"Fran-Mex Inversion Financing Corporation, S. A."

"Which is?"

"Some Ali somebody who's living in Argentina or somewhere."

"He had the damned gall to come to you? Right! Even with my experience, I can't believe that!"

"It seems he hired somebody as incompetent as he is. He

didn't contact me, himself."

"You gonna find him an investor or two?"

"Yeah! I already found one! Ahmad! He puts in a million cash, up front, and gets to meet the one looking for financing."

"Gonna arrange it?"

"Why not? Nobody told me not to! I can use a couple million, right now. I lost that much on a recent deal. The timing's just right."

Clint laughed and hung up.